Fancy NANCY
and the Fabulous Fashion Boutique

Written by Jane O'Connor   Illustrated by Robin Preiss Glasser

HARPER
An Imprint of HarperCollinsPublishers

For Robin, who brought banana walking
into my life, and so much more!
—J. O'C.

For my Russian ballet teacher, Mademoiselle Seda, whose handmade costumes are,
forty years later, influencing Nancy's fashion decisions
—R.P.G.

Fancy Nancy and the Fabulous Fashion Boutique
Text copyright © 2010 by Jane O'Connor
Illustrations copyright © 2010 by Robin Preiss Glasser
All rights reserved. Printed in the United States of America.
No part of this book may be used or reproduced in any manner whatsoever without written permission except in the case
of brief quotations embodied in critical articles and reviews. For information address HarperCollins Children's Books,
a division of HarperCollins Publishers, 10 East 53rd Street, New York, NY 10022.
www.harpercollinschildrens.com

Library of Congress Cataloging-in-Publication Data
O'Connor, Jane.
    Fancy Nancy and the fabulous fashion boutique / written by Jane O'Connor : illustrated by Robin Preiss
Glasser.—1st ed.
        p.   cm.
    Summary: Nancy sets up a fabulous fashion boutique to earn money to buy herself a beautiful fuchsia fan,
and the items she was selling come in handy when her sister's birthday party goes awry.
    ISBN 978-0-06-123592-4 (trade bdg.) — ISBN 978-0-06-123593-1 (lib. bdg.)
    ISBN 978-0-06-202601-9 (special ed.)
    [1. Moneymaking projects—Fiction.   2. Parties—Fiction.   3. Sisters—Fiction.   4. Vocabulary—Fiction.]
I. Preiss-Glasser, Robin, ill.   II. Title.
PZ7.O222Fhp 2010   2010007820
[E]—dc22   CIP
                                                                                AC

Typography by Jeanne L. Hogle
10 11 12 13 14   CG/WOR   10 9 8 7 6 5 4 3 2 1
❖
First Edition

It's my sister's birthday on Saturday, so we are going on a shopping spree. That means we're buying balloons, napkins, party plates, cups—a ton of stuff!

My sister and Freddy are only interested in pirates, pirates, pirates.... They're completely obsessed!

When she's not looking, I get my sister the perfect present—a black eye patch.

On the way home my mom agrees to stop at Belle's Fabulous Fashion Boutique. Last week I saw the most beautiful lace fans there.

Ooh la la! One of the fans is on the bargain table. But I spent nearly all my money on my sister's present.

Then I get an idea that is brilliant. (That's fancy for supersmart.)
I will open my own fabulous fashion boutique and sell some
of my old gowns and accessories. Everything will be a bargain!
If I make enough money, that lace fan will be mine.

We set up the boutique in our front yard.
My sister and Freddy carry signs for the
grand opening.

Voilà! My first customers arrive—Rhonda and Wanda from across the street. "Welcome to my boutique," I say. "That's French for fancy store."

"Do you have any dresses with ruffles?" Rhonda asks.

Do I? Practically every dress in my boutique has ruffles! "Follow me to the dressing room," I say.

Dressing Room

"Oh, that looks stunning on you," I tell Rhonda. "It matches your eyes!"

Rhonda says she'll take it.

Ooh la la! My first sale!

Wanda likes one of the necklaces.

"It's made of rhinestones. Rhinestones are genuine fake diamonds," I explain.

Wanda says, "I'll come back after I get my allowance."

"No! She can't have it!
I want it!" my sister says.

I pretend not to hear. "Au revoir!" I wave to the twins.
More customers come. In practically no time I sell
a boa, a parasol, and two pairs of high heels.

The money is piling up!

Unfortunately business is much slower the next day. Freddy wants a red cape, but I explain that the Fashion Boutique does not accept chocolate coins.

Today! Even more good stuff!

My sister still wants the rhinestone necklace.
"Here!" She gives me a penny.

I try to make her understand. "The necklace costs way more than a penny.... And anyway, you like pirate stuff," I say. "Pirates don't wear rhinestone necklaces."

My sister does not understand—she throws a tantrum. A tremendous, gigantic, horrendous tantrum.

Sure enough, Wanda shows up
right then to buy the necklace.

Double ooh la la! I have enough money now
to buy the beautiful fan.

Later on, my sister catches me wrapping her birthday present.
"Is it the pretty necklace? Is it the pretty necklace?" she asks.
"It's a surprise" is all I say.

Suddenly I feel bad. I don't want her to be disappointed on her birthday.

I ask my dad to walk me over to the twins' house. "Is there any way I can persuade you to return the necklace?" I ask Wanda. (Persuade is fancy for getting somebody to do what you want.)

Here is what it takes to persuade Wanda. I give back her money <u>and</u> I give her two bracelets and a ring—for free! I guess I have to forget about the beautiful fan.

On Saturday morning my sister opens her presents.
She loves the eye patch ... and she is overjoyed (that's
super-duper happy) when she sees the necklace.

She is wearing them both when her guests arrive.

Look Out Tower

Dead End Forest

PIRATE HIDE OUT

The pirate treasure hunt has just begun when—uh-oh—it starts raining!

We all hurry inside.

The rain does not stop.
"What will we do now?" my sister asks. "My party is no fun."
"Hey, why don't we put on a fashion show!" I say.

Everyone dresses up in all the leftover stuff from my boutique. Then I race downstairs for bananas. **Why?**

Balancing a banana on your head makes you walk tall and straight like a model. I demonstrate—that's fancy for show—how to do it.

Banana
Walking:
1) Put banana
on head
2) Walk
tall!

Just like at a real fashion show, I describe each ensemble. "Ladies and gentlemen, doesn't this pirate queen look lovely in her royal blue evening gown?"

At the end, there is lots of applause.... That's fancy for clapping.

Now it's time for the cake. We all sing,
"**Happy birthday, dear JoJo . . .**"

"You are a wonderful big sister," my dad whispers to me.
I feel so happy, almost like it's my birthday too.

The next day there is a surprise—a big sister present.
It is the fan!

Don't you love happy endings?